For my parents, Michael and Kathi O'Sullivan,
who gave me the best place to live.

—K.G.

For my mom and uncle David.

—C.S.N.

If You Live Here
Text copyright © 2022 by Kate Gardner
Illustrations copyright © 2022 by Christopher Silas Neal
All rights reserved. Manufactured in Italy.
No part of this book may be used or reproduced in any manner whatsoever without written permission except in the case of brief quotations embodied in critical articles and reviews. For information address HarperCollins Children's Books, a division of HarperCollins Publishers, 195 Broadway, New York, NY 10007.
www.harpercollinschildrens.com

ISBN 978-0-06-286532-8

The artist used mixed media to create the illustrations for this book.
Typography by Dana Fritts
21 22 23 24 25  RTLO  10 9 8 7 6 5 4 3 2 1

First Edition

# If You Live Here

Written by
## Kate Gardner

Illustrated by
## Christopher Silas Neal

BALZER + BRAY
*An Imprint of HarperCollinsPublishers*

If you live in a
tree house . . .

you'll need to
be a good listener.

If you live on a spaceship,

keep curious, for there
is wonder all around.

If you live on a train,

you know that everything changes.

If you live in a burrow,
everyone snuggles.

If you live in a castle,
the view is better when
shared with friends.

If you live in a candy store—
you might grow tired of candy.

If you live in a garden,
your patience will be rewarded.

If you live on a farm,
you'll see all kinds of families
each day.

ANIMAL FARM

If you live in a dollhouse,
you will have to become
very little indeed!

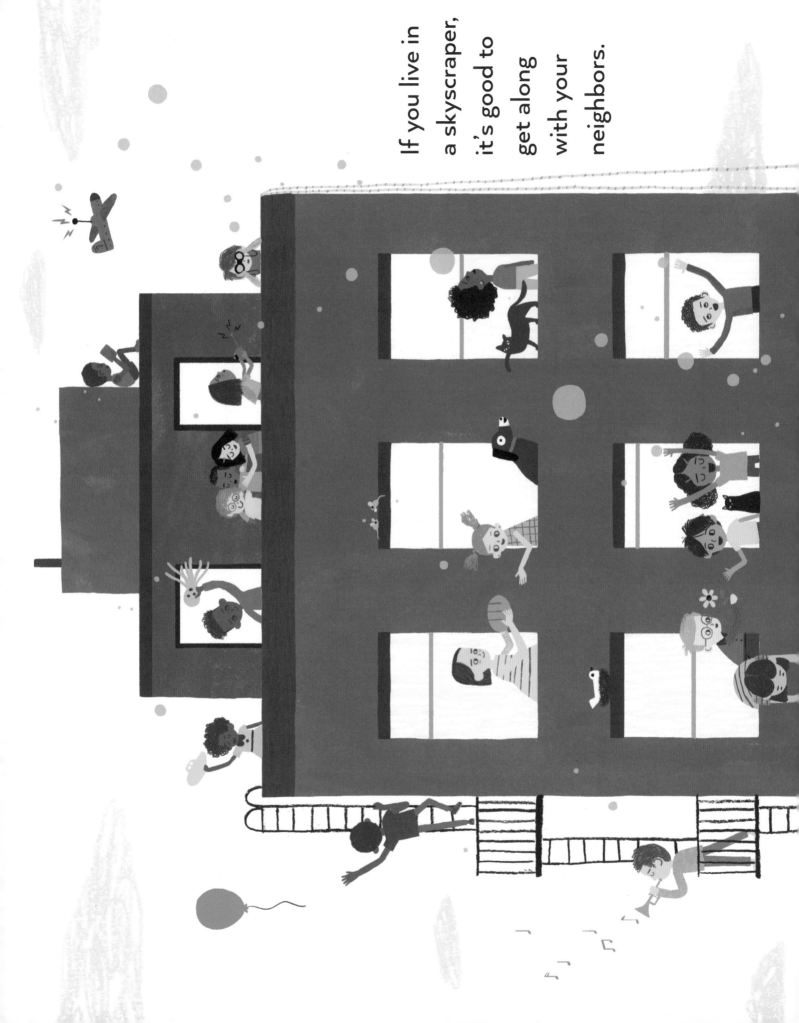

If you live in a skyscraper, it's good to get along with your neighbors.

If you live in a submarine,
you must like strange visitors.

The opposite is true
if you live in a lighthouse.

If you live in a nest,
you need to be ready to leave
when it's time.

If you live in a house,
may you have many books
and nooks in which to read them.

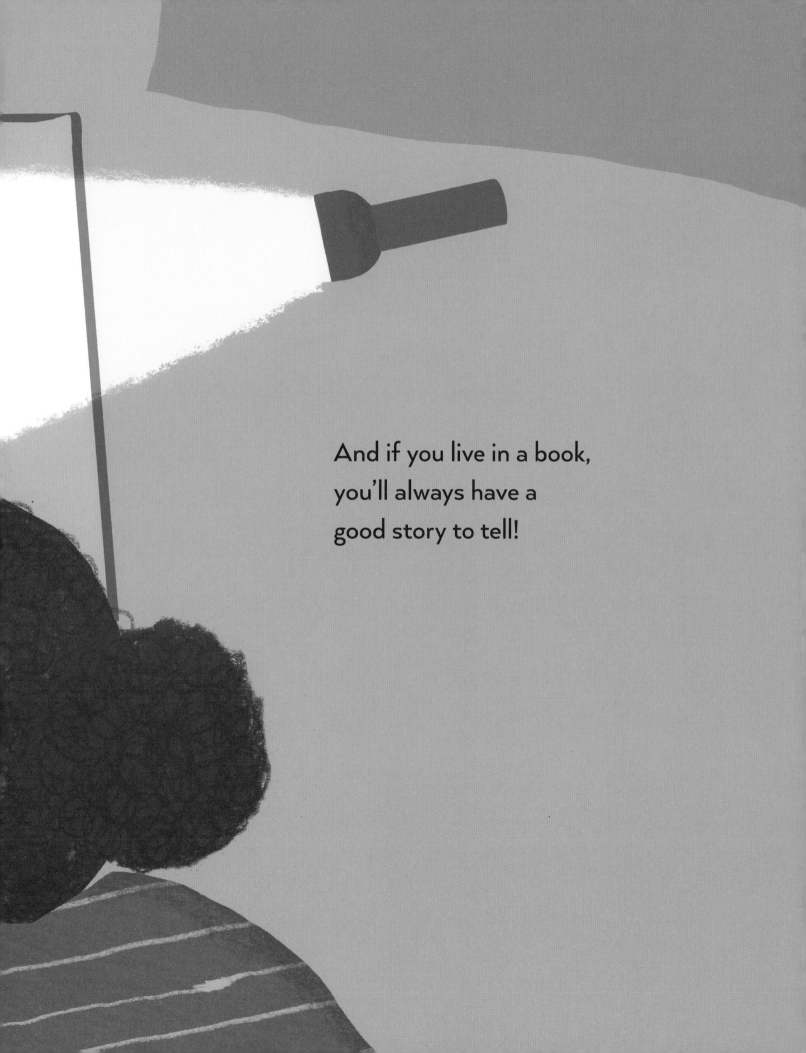

And if you live in a book,
you'll always have a
good story to tell!